The Birthday cake

Text and illustrations by
Sven Nordqvist

Opal

There once was an old man called Pettson who had a cat named Findus. They lived in a little red house with a toolshed and a henhouse and a woodshed and an outside loo and a garden. Round about there were fields and meadows and, a little farther away the forest.

They said that Pettson was crazy. People talk so much you don't know what to believe. It is true he was forgetful and absent-minded sometimes. He wasn't quite like other people, walking about alone talking to the cat. That would not have been so bad either if it had not been for what Mr Gustavsson told everybody about Pettson's pancake mix. And about him climbing over the roof to get to the shop. And about him tying a curtain to the cat's tail. Gustavsson had seen that himself so it had to be true. If you go around behaving like that, you just have to be crazy, don't you?

All the things that made people talk about Pettson so much happened on Findus' birthday. Findus had birthdays three times a year, just because it was more fun that way. Every time the cat had a birthday, Pettson baked him a birthday cake out of pancakes.

As usual Pettson had been in the henhouse that morning and filled a whole basket full of eggs. And now he was sitting on the bench outside the kitchen door, polishing the eggs. They had to be all nice and clean because Pettson wanted to do everything in the proper way. Findus paced impatiently up and down the bench, waiting for the pancake baking to start.

"Is it necessary to polish all the eggs NOW?" said the cat irritatedly. "I'll have time for another birthday before the cake's ready."
"You're so impatient," said the old man. "We'll just have to start rightaway then. We'll take three eggs into the kitchen and we'll see if there's going to be a cake."
" 'Course there's going to be a cake," said Findus. He was already in the kitchen looking for the pan. The rest of the eggs were left in the basket on the bench.

Pettson broke the eggs into a bowl.
"Now we need milk and sugar and a little salt and butter and flour," he said taking the things from the larder. But he could not find the flour.
"Where's the flour? Have you eaten all the flour, Findus?" he called from the larder.
"I certainly have not eaten all the flour," said Findus indignantly.
"Must have done it myself then," muttered the old man, scratching his nose thoughtfully. He looked another three times through the whole larder, in the woodstowe, the wardrobe and the chest but he could not find any flour.
"I'll have to bike down to the shop and buy some flour, then. You wait here, I'll soon be back," said Pettson to the cat and went out to get his blue bike. But the cat did not want to wait there and he dashed out before the old man.

Just as Pettson was about to ride off on his bike, he noticed that the back tyre was flat.
"What's this now? Did you bite a hole in the tyre, Findus?" the old man complained
in a temper.
I certainly never bite holes in tyres," replied the cat indignantly.
"Must have done it myself, then," mumbled the old man worriedly pulling his ear.
"But it doesn't matter. I'll soon fix it. Just you wait here and I'll fetch some tools from
the shed. Then I'll mend the puncture and I'll bike to the shop and buy some flour so
we can get on with your birthday cake."
But the cat did not want to wait there and ran to the shed before him.

But just as Pettson was about to open the door to the shed, the key was missing and the door could not be opened.

"What's the meaning of this?" the old man moaned sulkily. "This door's never locked. Is it you who's lost the key, Findus?"

"I certainly do not lose keys," replied the cat very indignantly.

"Must have done it myself, then. That was a nuisance indeed," groused the old man, thoughtfully poking his eye. To make sure, he peered in through the window. Then he tried the door again but it was still locked.

Then Findus whistled from the well, and pointed down. Pettson hurried over to him.
"Oh, look, there's the key, right at the bottom. How did it get there? And how am I
to get it out?" He pulled his lip and gave the matter some lengthy thought until his
whole body jumped when he hit on the answer.
"I know! If I put a hook on a long stick, I'll be able to fish the key out. Have you got
a long stick Findus?"
"I have certainly never had a long stick," said Findus, not knowing if he should be
indignant.
"Must have one myself somewhere then," the old man mused, scratching his hat.
"Just you wait here and I'll go and find one. Then I'll fish out the key and we'll get
into the shed so I can fetch the tools and mend the bike so I can ride to the shop and
buy some flour so we can get on with your birthday cake."
But the cat did not want to wait there and ran ahead of him to look.

So Pettson and his cat looked
everywhere for a long stick . They
looked in the henhouse, behind the
toolshed, in the garden, in the woodshed, behind the best sofa and in the
larder but nowhere did they find a long
stick, not until Pettson remembered that
he had a long fishing rod in the loft of
the toolshed.

"The fishing rod will do fine," thought Pettson. "Just have to get the ladder first and climb over the roof and in through the skylight. But the ladder's behind the woodshed in Andersson's field and that's where Anderssons bad-tempered bull is too, asleep and using the ladder as a pillow. So I daren't go in and get it because he'll wake up and go mad. We'll have to trick him into moving first somehow. How can we do that, though?" Pettson raked his beard and thought so hard you could hear his brain ticking over.

"Are you good at bullfighting?" The old man asked Findus after a lengthy ponder.

"No, no. Never fought a single bull," replied Findus alarmed.

"Pity," said Pettson worriedly, "because if we can't trick the bull into moving, I can't fetch the ladder and then I can't get the fishing rod down from the loft and then I can't get into the shed and get my tools and then I can't mend the bike and then I can't ride to the shop and buy some flour and then there'll be no birthday cake. And what sort of a birthday will it be if we can't have a birthday cake?"
Findus sat in silence for a while. Then he said: "I've made the odd cow or two run, though, of course. So I should be able to get that old bull to run too at a pinch."
"Yes, I thought as much. Feeling the pinch in your stomach now, are you?" said Pettson, peering at the cat knowingly. "Maybe the fastest cat in the world is a bit lazy sometimes. I'll just go and fetch some things now and then we'll get that bull running. You just wait here and I'll be straight back," he said and went into the house.

In the kitchen the old man took down one of the red and yellow flowered curtains and from the sitting room he fetched the gramophone with the hornshaped loudspeaker and a record. Then he went back out to the cat and tied the curtain to his tail.

"They have a curtain like this when they bull-fight in Spain," said Pettson. "Now don't run off before I give the word!" Then off he went and put the gramophone at the gate to the field where Andersson's bull stood sleeping. He put the record on and wound the gramophone up. It was another old man named Jussi Björling who was singing a song called "To sea". "This should wake anyone up," chuckled the old man delightedly.

When the sound blared out of the horn and out over the field, the bull first took a few sleepy steps back and forth, settled his head on the rung of the ladder and went back to sleep because the singer on the record held back a little at the beginning. But, afterwards, when he was giving it all he got, the bull really moved.

He woke with a jump straight into the air, staring in alarm all round. "What, what was that?" He looked more and more irritated and glowered fiercely at a passing bumblebee. No, it wasn't that, it came from behind somewhere. He span round, caught sight of Pettson and the cat and the gramophone and bellowed: "There it is, take that din away or else I'll do it myself!" and he lowered his head, stepping back and forth to gain a firm foothold. He tensed all his muscles, braced himself for the charge and with a toss of the head thundered towards Pettson and Findus and the gramophone.

"Now!" whispered Pettson to the cat. "Run for all you're worth." And Findus shot off like a comet with the red and yellow-flowered curtain flapping from his tail. When the bull saw this, he turned sharply round and chased it because he was so drowsy and bad-tempered that he thought it was the curtain blaring out the awful noice.

When they had made it halfway across the field, Pettson hurriedly crawled under the gate. He quickly fetched the ladder and crawled back again. Just then, the cat came back at tremendous speed with the yellow curtain trailing behind him.

The bull, who was completely exhausted from the chase, stood panting at the far end of the field, wondering what had happened.

But Findus kept going anyway, propelled by the sheer speed, past the bench outside the kitchen door where the egg basket stood. The curtain caught on the basket, turned it over and all the eggs rolled into a puddle. In the next instant Pettson had also got caught up in the curtain, tripped and sat right on the eggs. Not an egg was left unbroken.

Pettson let out a stream of bad language, struggled up and glowered at the sticky mess.

"Why did you put the egg basket on the bench, Findus? Look at this now!" he ranted.

"I certainly did not put any eggs on a bench," the cat hissed offended.

"Must have done it myself then," the old man hissed back. Then he calmed down because it was Findus' birthday.

"This is terrible," he sighed. "I'll have to clean up a bit before I get on with your birthday cake because I like to do things properly."

So he took a shovel and started to scoop up the muddy, eggy mess into a slop bucket.

At this point Gustavsson arrived.

"Hello, Pettson. Working hard as usual, I see," said Gustavsson, peering curiously at the eggy mess.

"Well, not much of that getting done today," Pettson answered. "We're celebrating a birthday, you see, so I'm making the pancake mix. I thought I'd bake us a really nice cake. He scooped up the last of the eggy mud from the puddle.

"There we are," he said stretching and wiping his hands on the seat of his trousers. Then he felt that the trousers were all eggy and sticky. "It's about time I treated myself to a new pair of trousers, anyway. These are more than thirty years old," he thought, taking them off.

"We'll throw these in as well. If you have birthdays only three times a year, you should have a real celebration," he said, pressing the trousers down into the bucket. Gustavsson just stared at the sludge in the bucket. Pancake mix! He cast a sideways glance cautiously at Pettson. The old man must have gone crazy. The best thing to do is pretend not to notice.

"I see. A pancake birthday cake for you and the cat. Sounds good!" said Gustavsson trying to sound encouraging.

"I'll say, my own recipe," said Pettson looking proud. "But first I have to go to the shop and buy some flour. Wait here a while and I'll soon be back." He took the ladder and went over to the toolshed, climbed up and disappeared over the other side of the roof.

Gustavsson stood looking up at the roof for a few moments. Then he looked at the muddy eggy mess in the bucket and at the cat pacing impatiently back and forth with a red and yellow-flowered curtain tied to its tail and at the wind-up gramophone that had got stuck and was wailing "– seeea, tooooo sea – seeea, tooooo sea – seeea, tooooo sea –". Then he looked up at the roof again where Pettson had disappeared. "The shop's in the other direction," he said in a quiet voice. Then he turned and went home. He looked as if he was deep in thought.

From that day on, everyone in the area thought Pettson had gone crazy. But Findus did not think so. Because after Pettson had crawled in through the skylight to the loft of the toolshed, he soon found the fishing rod. Then he climbed down again and bent on a steel wire hook to the end of the rod and then he went to the well and fished out the key. Then he opened the door to the toolshed and got his tools and mended the puncture and rode the bike to the shop and bought some flour and new trousers and rode home again and baked a mouth-watering birthday cake for Findus.

Then they sat in the garden, drinking coffee and eating cake and playing Viennese waltzes on the wind-up gramophone, just as they usually did when Findus had a birthday.
Pettson wasn't so crazy at all.